SHE LAUGHS LAST

ORPHAN DREAMER SAGA
Episode Three
A Short Story: Grandma Gertrude and Nomed

J. NELL BROWN

Orphan Dreamer Saga: Episode Three
She Laughs Last: A Short Story

Published by J. Nell Brown, LLC and Rogue Reads, LLC

"We Wear the Mask"
Words by Paul Laurence Dunbar, 1872-1906
Public Domain

For ordering information, contact the publisher via the author's website, www.JNellBrown.com.

Printed in the United States of America.

First Edition, 2019

BOOKS BY
J. Nell Brown

NONFICTION

Shhh, My Father Is Speaking, and I Am Listening: A Bible Study on Hearing God's Voice

Blood Moon—God's Warning: Why Knowledge of Jewish Feasts Is Essential to Understand the Blood Moons of 2014 and 2015

FICTION

Orphan Dreamer Saga
Orphan Dreamer and the Missing Arrowhead

Orphan Dreamer and the Glass Tattoo

She Laughs Last

Orphan Tree: Rooted in Eternal Love

Collector's First Edition Paperback
The Omega Journey: Blood Moons Whisper

COMING SOON

A Generation of Lighted Evergreens

Orphan Falls: Wild and Free

House Guest

Orphan Star: The Mark

Little Peach Lies

Orphan's Seed

If Love's a Fish

Orphan's Horizon

Orphan's End

What sorrow awaits you who laugh now,
for your laughing will turn to mourning and
sorrow.

—Luke 6:25

"We Wear the Mask" by Paul Laurence Dunbar

We wear the mask that grins and lies,
It hides our cheeks and shades our eyes,
This debt we pay to human guile;
With torn and bleeding hearts we smile,
And mouth with myriad subtleties

Why should the world be over-wise,
In counting all our tears and sighs?
Nay, let them only see us, while
We wear the mask.

We smile, but, O great Christ, our cries
To thee from tortured souls arise.
We sing, but oh the clay is vile
Beneath our feet, and long the mile;
But let the world dream otherwise,
We wear the mask!

1—Grandmothers Can Lie Too

July 7, 1981
Georgia

SHE WHO LAUGHS LAST WINS: true or false?

Sandwiching man and woman between the first and the fourth dimensions, the universe suffocates its human prey before consuming it. Promising light beyond the darkness and truths that are nothing more than lies, it laughs last—for now.

Laughter.

A lie.

Tears.

The truth.

We wear the mask.

It fits, so we wear it well.

2—Grandmothers Can Lie Too

SHE WOULDN'T MISS IT FOR the world, even though the soon-to-be grandmother's least favorite time of day had arrived. Nightfall. The sun hides on the other side of Earth, while the moon makes a paltry attempt to replace the sun's blazing presence, casting a swath of pale blue-white light across North America.

Her back ballerina straight, Mrs. Gertrude Smith has been sitting smack-dab in the middle section of a Greyhound bus for the last six hours. Tapping her right foot, she adjusts her crocheted shawl, securing the coverlet around her slight shoulders to hide the goosebumps popping up across her arms—the evidence of her fear. She curves her lips into a smile—a mask—determined to conceal her truth from the other passengers.

The driver keeps the bus moving at a constant speed, while the Greyhound charges south down I-75 toward Gainesville, Florida. The swamp.

Breathe.

Just breathe.

Almost out of Georgia.

Born and raised in just another dried-up farm town in America—Chadbourn, North Carolina—Mrs. Smith rummages through her carpetbag, looking for a worthy distraction. She finds it in a paperback, discovered at a book depository in Whiteville, North Carolina. Like a schoolgirl playing hooky during a boring class, she hunkers down, shines a flashlight on yellowed pages, and reads the fancy scientist's wisdom in *Questions about the Universe*.

> The first dimension gives the universe its length: the x-axis. The second dimension describes its height: the y-axis. And together, the x-axis and the y-axis form a square. The third dimension, known as the z-axis, describes the depth of the universe, giving an object area and even cross-section as illustrated in the properties of a cube. Look at a cube and note that it possesses three dimensions—length, width, depth—and thus, volume. The fourth dimension represents time. Time governs the properties of all other matter at any given point in the universe.

"I've got it, Mister Science-man." Widowed for the last ten years, Mrs. Smith had gotten used to talking to herself and keeping herself company. Fortunately, the passenger sitting in the window seat next to her didn't mind and chimed in to the conversation.

"Got what, ma'am?"

"What the professor's trying to say in this book, *Questions about the Universe*."

"Well, what's he saying?"

"Time is the boss lady of the other three dimensions, no different than I'm the boss lady of my farm."

"Oh. You own your own farm?"

"I do."

"Farming I understand. Never owned one, but I grew up in South Carolina. There was cotton for days. But . . . dimensions? I don't have a clue what you're going on about."

"Neither do I. At least not completely." Mrs. Smith chuckles as she closes her book and removes her reading glasses, giving her eyes a rest.

"Where are you traveling?"

"Florida."

"Family?"

"First grandbaby's on the way."

"Ahh. The first. So special."

"Special. Magical. A dreamer." Her voice drops to a whisper. "A child who will bend time." *But what exactly does bending time mean?* Mrs. Smith rubs her fingers across the book's cover, hoping it will answer her question. "Tibet promised Austin, my son-in-law, that our grandbaby would be special."

"We've got one of those in our family. A five-year-old boy trapped in a sixteen-year-old's body. He's a sweet kid."

"Are you a grandmother?"

"Seven times over. I can see you're already so proud of her even though you ain't even met her. That's a grandma's love."

A grandmother's love. Tenacious. Soft. Unforgettable. Mrs. Smith lifts her chin, basking in the sunlight of her own maternal pride. After rubbing her eyes, she opens her book and continues reading.

> The other dimensions are where deeper possibilities—even alternate realities—may come into play. But explaining the existence of additional dimensions can be tricky. According to the Superstring Theory, inside the fifth dimension, and perhaps even the sixth dimension, other worlds may exist. If a human could see through these dimensions, could we travel back in time or explore different versions of the future?

Time travel? What if a person gets lost and can't find her way back? Mrs. Smith's heart pounds against her ribs like a monster begging to be released from prison.

Bending time, even realities. That's what Tibet had promised.

"But how?" She slaps her hand across her mouth. Passengers shoot daggers at her from behind their bloodshot eyes. "Excuse me. Didn't mean to disturb." A scowl fades from the passenger's face who sits across the aisle, but Mrs. Smith's question persists.

How would her granddaughter—the descendent of sharecroppers, slaves, preachers, teachers, and farmers—distort something as powerful as time?

"How many dimensions are there?" she asks out loud, as though the author of the book is sitting beside her.

"Ten . . . that we know of." The man with the fading scowl points at her book. "I wrote it."

She gasps. "Professor Albert?"

"That's me. In the flesh."

"N-n-nice to meet you, sir." Mrs. Smith nods as she clutches a handful of her paisley dress. "I've never met a professor before. That is, until my Jeanette went off to Spelman College."

"Well, how do you do, Missus . . . ?"

"Smith. Just fine, sir." She clears her throat. "Why are you riding the bus, Professor?"

"Is it a crime?"

"I mean . . . it's just that usually a well-off white man owns a car and drives himself wherever he wants to go."

"I own a car, but I can't drive." She wants to ask why, but that would be rude. "Multiple sclerosis. My legs are too weak to drive." He quells her curiosity with nine words.

"But your mind is still strong."

"For now. My memory's going the way of my legs—south." He chuckles, hiding his pain. He wears a mask too. "If you have any questions about the universe and its dimensions, ask. I'll try to remember what I wrote."

"Thank you, sir." Mrs. Smith's heart flutters. How can she help the man? Even a rich man can be unfortunate.

Maybe a Greyhound bus heading South isn't as dangerous as she'd thought.

A few seconds later, the answer to her question about bending time comes in the form of a deep knowing. The answer is simple: her granddaughter would learn how to bend time—and thus, her reality—by tapping into a source of power higher than the fourth dimension, something or someone omniscient, all-knowing, all-wise, and all-seeing, not limited by the constructs of time. The great I AM. Ever present in humanity's past, present, and future.

Another question lingers. The professor won't know the answer to that question, so she whispers a prayer, "Promise me. Don't take my grandbaby too."

3—Grandmothers Can Lie Too

MRS. SMITH ADJUSTS HER MASK, hiding behind a glaze of faux smiles and feigned bravery while she fiddles with the frayed edges of her shawl. The professor glances at her, and she forces a smile across her mahogany face—but her mouth dries and a cold sweat drips down the nape of her neck, slithering down her back.

It's not the 1960s anymore.

You're okay.

But she isn't okay now—and she wasn't okay back then. Neither was her son, James.

Oblivious of her silent fears, the bus driver shuttles her

deeper and deeper into the Southern night. Goin' down the river, as the old folks used to say.

"Mister Driver, don't stop—not for nothing and no one," she says beneath her breath. Her slender frame shudders, but she must act brave and swallow her fears, because in less than twenty-four hours, her only surviving child, Jeanette Cavanaugh, would give birth to a baby girl, transforming Mrs. Gertrude Smith into Grandma Gertrude.

A baby. A new life, with new dreams all wrapped up inside velvet-soft skin. New hope. New possibilities—and no demon roaming Earth would be stopping that plan. She prays that her hopes won't mimic those Russian dolls with their hidden layers.

Like a deception masquerading beneath a smiling face—and sometimes, even a laugh.

But still a lie.

Fathered by the prince of lies—the Prince of Power of the Air—before he hid his truth beneath the veneer of fake joviality, all tucked between the first and the fourth dimensions of the universe.

Be brave.

Mrs. Smith dabs her face with a lace handkerchief, removing any signs of pain and making sure her tears don't melt her mask.

4—Nomed

One Cosmic Revolution
Immortals—Time without End

DECEPTION. LIES. MISPLACED JOVIALITY. IT is his modus operandi, and so it remains the devil's business to convince a human to laugh at another's misfortune. Demons always laugh, but that doesn't mean they are happy.

Nomed waits in a cold cave, which is rather ironic because he's in hell.

Tsk tsk. Don't pity him.

After the moon drips with blood, he will come for you. Until then, Nomed lives at his summer residence, prepping for his meeting with humanity: Armageddon, the day he will scrub Earth clean of its invaders—you, and that girl, the Orphan Dreamer, the one who bends time, sticking her big nose where it doesn't belong.

Nomed's plan?

It's simple: doubt.

Doubt in God's love leads to hopelessness, then depression, and finally death by suicide. Nomed finishes the blueprint of his war plans and lays down his pencil. Armageddon, the war that will finish off the Orphan Dreamer.

Her end, his beginning.

Nomed smirks. Leaning back against the frigid wall of granite, he laughs until the sun sets and the moon shines. Because when the Orphan Dreamer dies, who will protect Earth's intruders—you—from Nomed and his army coming to reclaim what they once ruled?

Time's up.

Moving day has arrived.

5—Grandmothers Can Lie Too

July 7, 1981
Georgia

MRS. SMITH CLUTCHES HER PAISLEY carpetbag to her chest. The bag's tattered fabric protects two priceless gifts: a small weathered mirror and a patchwork quilt that hides a secret map within its patterns.

Promising safety within the darkness, sleep lures Mrs. Smith to rest, but she refuses to close her eyes. The *Negro Motorist Green Book* suggests that danger lurks in the shadows of highways for even alert passengers meandering deep into the South—and that danger increases for unsuspecting and sleeping travelers.

If a monster with two legs and two arms was going to

beat her with iron pipes, hammers, and chains, she would be awake.

The beating.

Followed by screams.

Rivulets of blood.

And even death.

Her body trembles. *Please, God. Don't force me to remember.* Bitterness sours her breath. Eyes heavy, Mrs. Smith gazes past the window at the night sky. Moonlight breaks past a bank of low-hanging clouds, casting shadows down the spines of gangly pines.

What she wouldn't give for a touch of the professor's mental fogginess. She had broken her promise, and broken promises demand payment. Since that dreadful day—May 14, 1961—Mrs. Smith had refused to ride any Greyhound or Trailways bus ever again.

No matter what.

Then, six months ago, the phone rang.

"Momma."

"Jeanette! How's my little girl?"

"Forty plus, and guess what?

"Give me some good news, Tiger."

"Momma, this summer, you're going to become a grandma."

A grandmother. That was good news, until she remembered that Austin and Jeanette lived in Florida, and she lived in North Carolina. Too far to walk and no car to drive. Only mode of transportation left: a bus ride.

"I'm sorry, son." Gertrude squeezes her eyes shut, and the fateful memories flood her mind. *Dear God!* She bites down on her lower lip to keep herself from screaming. *Why didn't you protect him? You run out of angels?*

It is a truth not always universally acknowledged that no hardworking, tax-paying American teenager deserved such a beating. He had purchased that ticket at regular price, believing it earned him the right to sit somewhere besides the back of a bus. But the group of homegrown American terrorists who invaded the bus station in Anniston, Alabama, believed differently. It was only twenty years ago that an angry mob of three hundred beat the brains out of those Freedom Riders in the land of the free and the brave—America.

That bloodthirsty mob almost beat James to death right then and there.

Seven days later, he died at home, in his mother's arms. Mrs. Smith cries softly as she remembers her son. "James," she says, the words barely crossing her lips.

"Miss." A familiar voice jars her back into the present. She sniffs hard and wipes her face with the back of her hand before facing the professor.

"Sir?"

"Are you okay?"

"I'm just fine, sir." Smiling, she dons the mask again, wearing it well. But inside, the truth screams, "Jesus, don't you take my granddaughter!"

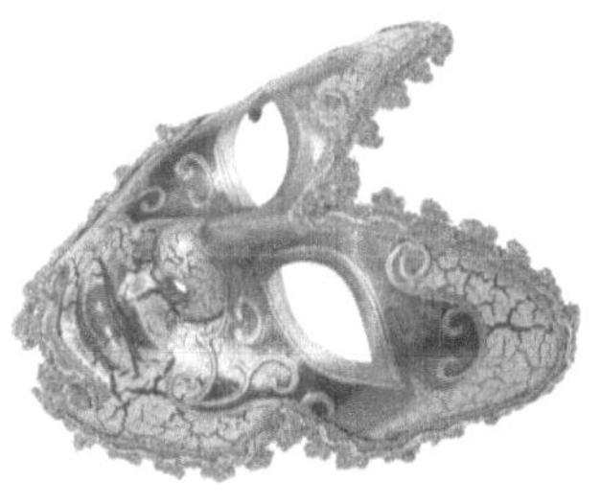

6—Nomed

ONE BLACK WING, TIPPED WITH metal hooks, pops through, followed by the other, as Nomed pushes himself into the unseen world—his rightful dimension—while wearing a smile bigger than the false grin of a human clown. He catches up to Yahweh's warrior, Legna. "I'd like to introduce you to my understudy."

A grotesque humpbacked creature with five legs and cyanotic purplish skin infected with oozing green pustules lumbers toward the two warriors "Her name is Aglaope. The humans call her depression. She's beautiful, isn't she?"

"Why is she here?"

"To visit the girl, your Orphan Dreamer."

"You'll never kill her."

"Don't intend to. Once depression finishes with Rose, she'll kill herself—then her dreams will perish, slaughtering everyone inside of them, including the Orphan."

"Aglaope's resume isn't flawless."

"You're forgetting the power of the inquisitor. If he convinces Rose's mother to doubt her child's sanity, could the Orphan Dreamer survive a mother's disbelief in her very essence—her reality?" Nomed shrieks a laugh. "No—never. Her hope will be wiped out by her own mother. With hope dead, Rose won't even fight back before she takes her own life. I've perfected the process; it works."

"She hasn't even been born yet." Legna rests his hand on the hilt of his sword.

"One day, she will be born. And I. Will. Be. There. Johnny-on-the-spot, as the humans say. I'll make her cry, alright. Without mercy, I'll rip her soul into shreds and make her weep. Because when tears are present, hopelessness always lurks nearby. Hopelessness proceeds despair. Despair begs for death, and I answer the cry of beggars."

"In your world of lies, laughter equals joy and tears equal pain; but lies are your truth, so how could you know the difference between what is true and what is false?" Legna walks away, then pauses. "Nomed."

"Miss me?"

"Hardly. I can smell you a universe away. Listen carefully."

"All ears."

"In the human's world, laughter can be heard even while they hide behind a mask. But no human can see another's tears unless the person crying chooses to remove their mask, revealing their vulnerability. Their truth."

"So what, Zorro?" Nomed laughs at his own joke.

"Not every laugh equals happiness, nor does every tear represent sadness."

"Legna. The warrior and the philosopher." Seething, Nomed returns to his hellish lair.

7—Grandmothers Can Lie Too

LIKE DARN NEAR EVERY OTHER Southern baby girl, Daniela Rose Cavanaugh was crying the moment she was born.

No.

Actually squalling. But ain't no sound more thrilling than the cries of a healthy newborn.

A girl.

A dreamer.

A warrior.

Grandma Gertrude Smith's first—and only—grandchild.

Hours after Jeanette's hysterectomy, Daniela's parents

sleep. Grandma Gertrude cradles Daniela in her arms, then kisses the baby's nose. "Just like a button." Daniela whimpers. "Life's gonna make you cry, Button. It's supposed to. But I'm going to make you smile if it's the last thing I do." No one and nothing are going to stand in the way of Grandma Gertrude's determination.

In the 1960s, when Southern women who looked like her didn't own anything except for aprons, mop buckets, and brooms, she had purchased her farm from the bank, making her a landowner.

"No crying gonna last forever. Joy comes in the morning." But the child keeps on wailing as though a demon is chasing her mind, planning to enslave her thoughts. "Ain't no devil gonna win this battle. No ifs, ands, or buts. You gonna die laughing, all the way to the pearly gates. Because at the finish line, you win, Button. Just wait and see." She whispers a prayer over her fretful granddaughter, Daniela Rose Cavanaugh, the Orphan Dreamer.

8—Grandmothers Can Lie Too

GRANDMOTHERS CAN AND DO LIE.

Grandma Gertrude's prophecy of a merry heart defining her granddaughter's demeanor proved to be a tall order for Daniela Rose. During her middle-school years, chaotic and negative thoughts imprisoned her mind, locking away any speck of joy in a Sing Sing prison kind of depression.

Concrete grey.

Not even a solitary stream of light peeked through its bars.

It was official. The reality of her condition became

entrenched in her when a psychiatrist diagnosed Daniela with depression and childhood-onset schizophrenia.

During recess, Daniela stands at the edge of the creek, watching a water moccasin slither through the water. She slides off her shoes and socks, then dips her right toe into the cold water. Would the snake's bite hurt? Would death come quickly?

The kids at school hate her. They say she's too smart or too dumb. Then what is she?

Alone.

Ever since she could remember, she has hated the loneliness. She steps into the water and approaches the snake.

It stops, turns, and waits.

What about Daddy? He's sick. Mom? She'd miss her. Her reflexes ignore the warning growing in her mind. She strides toward her choice of death.

"Stop!" Her teacher calls from the field behind her, but the determined child sloshes through the stream closer to the snake. The moccasin rears back. She swallows air. *Maybe this isn't such a swell idea.* Her foot slides over a smooth rock hidden in the creek bed. Losing her balance, she crashes into the pond. The snake floats inches from her head and rises above the water's surface, ready to strike.

Someone splashes into the water beside Daniela's shoulder. Hands grip her arms, pulling her from the creek. "What on earth are you doing?"

Daniela's shoulders start shaking. "I . . . I'm sorry, Mrs. Bender. I . . . I'm so sad."

"What are you saying?"

The little girl wags her head, then falls into her teacher's embrace.

"You listen to me and listen real good. Before you were born, Yahweh tucked away great plans for you. Your kindred friend will come. Just you wait and see."

"Yes, ma'am." Rose smiles, slipping her mask back on.

9—NOMED

LAUGHING, NOMED FACES HIS MASTER, the Prince of the Power of the Air. "She's a girl, and a stupid one at that. What twelve-year-old throws down a gauntlet at Death's feet and wins?"

"Her mother did."

"I forgot, my lord." Nomed bows low.

"See that Death wins this time."

"Kill her?"

Lucifer smiles. "You wanted a promotion—more time on Earth. Earn it."

"You're generous, master."

"Don't forget it."

10—Orphan Dreamer

SHE'S GONE. LEFT WITHOUT DANIELA'S permission.

Moss drips off sprawling oaks, gifting shade to the small group of mourners. Daniela's sweaty hands threaten to slip from her dad's grip on the right and her mom's trembling hand on the left. She tightens her squeeze as pallbearers lower her kindred spirit—her Grandma Gertrude—into a vault of cold earth.

With a gravelly voice, a man leads the mourners as they sing "Precious Lord, Take My Hand," followed by "Nearer My God to Thee." After the musical selection ends, Deaconess Brown sings more than speaks her eulogy, sounding like a female version of Dr. Martin Luther King Jr. "Gertrude was my friend. A mighty woman of God . . ."

But in Daniela's mind, there is a different scene playing. An orchestra of violins, cellos, and basses replay an ethereal, rich and breathy rendition of "Nearer My God to Thee" as she stands on the doomed deck of the RMS *Titanic*. The sea's salty breath sprays her face and whispers, "Sorry, miss. Time's up. You're going to drown."

Button.

That's what Daniela's grandmother had nicknamed her, and she cherished the name. How long before Daniela would see her Grandma Gertrude again? One raindrop thumps Daniela on the nose. Followed by another. Until, eventually, rain showers her face and soaks her clothes and hair. Everyone is drenched.

"Daniela."

"Yes, ma'am?" She looks up at her mother.

"I didn't say anything, Bumblebee." Her mom opens an umbrella over her head and nestles Daniela beneath it.

"I thought you called me."

"I didn't."

"Daniela." The grieving child looks left, then right, then finally over her shoulder, trying to find the source of the gentle, feminine voice. Pallbearers toss more dirt into the black hole.

"Daniela." It's getting a bit creepy. A voice with no face.

"Up here."

Daniela Rose looks up.

Grey clouds roll back. Sunrays split the sky, bathing the gravesite in amber hues. A voice seems to whisper, "Stop looking at your feet so much, Button. The Son's still shining on you." A grin pushes a smile wider than the Mississippi River in-between her cheeks.

Hope.

That's all she needed. Daniela's smile loosens into a giggle. The mourners glare at the awkward child, but she was used to people staring. Judging. Then finding her wanting. Their eyes say what their tongues refuse to speak. *What is wrong with you, girl? Your grandma's dead! Show some respect.*

But they were wrong, just like her mean-spirited classmates were wrong about Daniela. Grandma Gertrude is more alive than ever. "See you soon, Grandma."

Laughter.

Lies.

Smiling, she wipes a tear from her cheek, then slips her hand back into her mother's safe grip.

No need to act brave when she isn't. Daniela removes her mask. Another tear slips down her cheek.

Tears.

Truth.

The mourners stand still, staring, just watching Grandma Gertrude's only granddaughter—her legacy.

A chill creeps across the cemetery and settles beneath Daniela's skin.

A shadow passes in front of her, blurring the shapes of the leaves, branches, and mourners as though a glaze has been poured over her eyes. Leaves rustle, whispering an eerie call, "I'm coming for you, Rose."

Swallowing her fear, Daniela releases her parents' hands, removes the necklace from around her neck, and slips the ancient diamond—the Glass Tattoo—into her right hand. She makes a fist, clenching the stone.

Warm energy bursts into her palm, pulsing throughout her entire being. She opens her hand. The jewel has disappeared into her palm, leaving a beautiful blue snowflake tattoo.

"Be afraid, Rose." The shadow speaks, moving through the air between her face and its blurry form as though a hand is reaching out from a spider's web. Something dreadful, evil, and yet powerful abandons its own dimension and intrudes upon hers. A face scarier than a gargoyle's mug shot materializes directly in front of her. Its breath stinks of rotten eggs.

She stumbles backward, and her heart threatens to turn to stone. Do the other mourners see the monster?

No one screams or runs.

No. They don't see it. They're blind to its presence. Ignorance is bliss, until reality catches up with the ignorant.

Daniela stares at the beast, and it whispers another threat, "I am Death. Your grandmother—I took her. Miss her?"

"What do you think?" Daniela balls her hands into fists as tears from her raw emotion stain her mahogany cheeks. *Leave the watery stains. Don't hide.*

"I am your period. Your end. Your Armageddon. Be afraid of me, little girl."

She gazes at her grandmother's body's final resting place—a big black hole. Her stomach churns, and an ache throbs beneath her ribs.

"Button, you're a special girl, and don't you forget it." Her grandmother's words comfort her.

"I-I-I can do it, Grandma. I have to. F-f-for their sakes.

Not mine." She swallows hard, refusing to wipe away the tears, refusing to hide her truth: her loneliness, her pain, and her awkwardness.

The monster speaks again. "Don't even think about fighting me. You cannot win this war, Orphan Dreamer, a pathetic little cry baby. Lay down your weapon, and I may spare your life."

An icy dread slithers down her slight frame, enveloping her in a cold sweat. Daniela remembers her Grandma Gertrude's words, "You're not a slave to fear, Button. You're God's girl. His child."

I am Daniela.

I am brave.

I am Daniela.

I am brave.

Sunlight splashes across her face, drying her tears.

She straightens her back, raises her chin, and speaks to the monster. "You tell me to be afraid. Because you say that you will be my end, my Armageddon."

"Humans like warnings. A siren before a tornado. A receding tide before a tsunami rolls ashore."

Daniela Rose traces the edges of the Glass Tattoo inked into the palm of her right hand. She kisses the mark, accepting her destiny as the Orphan Dreamer—a journey of pain intermingled with hope, destiny mixed with the ordinary, and bravery amid evil's fight to fulfill her ultimate fear: the fear of being alone . . . forever.

"No, little boy. You're wrong." Through her tears, she whispers to the creature who dares to intrude into her dimension—her home, Earth, "I give you a warning."

"Me?"

"Yes. You, sir will learn to fear me." She steps forward, braving the assault of the beast's putrid stench blasting up her nose.

"Pray tell me, why?"

"Because I-I-I . . ."

"Cat scratched your tongue?"

Daniela's face flushes hot. She swallows hard then waits. *Help me.* Strength enters her voice. "I. Am. Armageddon—*your* end, a full stop—*your* period, *your* hell." Her lower lip trembles. More tears fall. Naked emotion stripped of any false bravery or beauty blurs her vision.

Still, she sees her future with enough clarity to know that where destiny leads her, the mask—formed from a clay of false joviality—will no longer fit. In her imagination, she clutches the edges of the mask with trembling hands and removes it, revealing her true self. Her vulnerabilities. Her fears mixed with bravery. Her faith sullied with doubt. Her joy mingled with pain. Her future influenced by the past.

One day, she will become the Orphan Dreamer. Wielding her weapon, the God Factor, she must defeat her invisible tormentor—the beast—or her parents will soon join her grandmother. Gone too soon.

Dark-grey clouds roll across the sky, blocking the sun's light once more. In the middle of summer, snow—not rain—falls from clouds pregnant with moisture, cloaking the soil in a wintry blanket.

Shivering, the mourners gasp but not Daniela. She lifts her chin and smiles. In time, frozen prayers—no different than snowflakes—eventually thaw, a winter yielding to spring. She whispers a prayer and a word of thanksgiving,

"Walk with me, Immanuel—God with us, like you walked with Grandma."

The monster forces a laugh from his contorted face, but a tear slips down his face. He knows that she realizes that she's not completely alone. Laughter. Lies. Tears. Lies. Again, he taunts the young warrior, the Orphan Dreamer. "Walk? No. You'll be running after I am finished with you."

Snow blows. Black clouds stumble over each other, but a miniscule ray of sunlight penetrates past the storm. Peace.

"Be very afraid of this storm, little girl."

"Why?"

"You cannot withstand the storm."

Daniela, the young warrior, glares into the intruder's eyes then speaks, "I am the storm."

Its form seizes as water gushes from beast's face, washing its vile image away.

Good riddance.

Daniela Rose wipes crystalized tears—snowflakes—from her cheeks, then laughs. Tears. Truth. Laughter. Truth. "One snowflake falls from heaven to quench hell's thirst." She gazes at the Glass Tattoo, the midnight-blue snowflake that stains the middle of her right palm. "I am that snowflake. I am Daniela. I am the Orphan Dreamer."

A misfit but still chosen.

The girl destined to force the beast to accept the truth— her truth, her reality. In the end, she wins. Everyone can win if they so choose. Because the Light has already won. The battle rages fierce, but the fight has been fixed. The beast, the dark shadow of death, has already lost, defeated by the Light.

"'O death, where is your victory? O grave, where is your sting?'"

Gone forever!

"'Even though I walk through the valley of the shadow of death, I will fear no evil, for you are with me.'" She studies the shifting shadows gyrating across the angry sky.

A shadow cannot form without a source of light and a source of darkness, but one day—the day of reckoning, the beast's Armageddon—the Light will obliterate the darkness. Shadows will cease to exist.

"Grandma, I'll be okay and so will you." A smile spread across Daniela's face, pushing dimples into honeyed-smooth and cinnamon-spiced cheeks. Standing ridgepole straight, Daniela Rose Cavanaugh gazes past the clouds, finding the Light. "After I'm finished with my to-do list down here, I'll walk with Immanuel through the valley of the shadow of death, and I'll join you on the other side where only the Light shines. Until then, I have to be brave, even in the shadows. Love you." She blows a kiss.

Crying, she laughs last.

—THE END—

Fate whispers, "You cannot withstand the storm." The warrior replies, "I am the Storm."

—Anonymous

Dear Reader,

Thoughtful reviews about an author's work are like a pay raise or a tip to employees in traditional jobs. If you enjoyed this short story—"She Laughs Last"—please take a moment to place a review wherever you purchased this short story, sharing with other readers what you've enjoyed. Your feedback is invaluable.

The A21 Campaign, a nonprofit organization to abolish the human trafficking of children, is my charity of choice. When you purchase a short story or novel in the Orphan Dreamer saga, ten percent of the profits will be donated to the A21 Campaign or organizations with a similar mission.

I look forward to saying hello to you on Facebook. Please like my page so you can keep up with my writing journey. Also, please sign up for my semiannual newsletter, and I will notify you about future releases, sales, and special events.

With gratitude,
J. Nell Brown

ORPHAN DREAMER AND THE MISSING ARROWHEAD

EPISODE ONE OF THE ORPHAN DREAMER SAGA

PROLOGUE

ONE YEAR BEFORE . . .
THURSDAY, APRIL 1, 1993
GAINESVILLE, FLORIDA

EVER SINCE I CAN REMEMBER, I have despised the loneliness, but I never asked for this kind of company.

Not then.

Not now.

Not ever.

It is true: I have begged God for a kindred spirit just like the deliciously independent orphan girl, Anne Shirley, who met and then fell into platonic love with Diana Barry—a beautiful crow-head girl—in Avonlea, the magical lands of *Anne of Green Gables*.

I am not anything to look at, but I am a crow-head. God drenched my curly locks with the same black ink that soaks a crow's wings, and for that bit of goodwill, I am grateful.

But I'm running out of time to find my elusive friend and gift her my homemade friendship bracelet—a chevron pattern of emerald weaved next to black, then plum and lavender, and finally yellow, before starting at emerald again.

Because one night, they will take me in order to save you.

My rafiki—"friend," a.k.a. my dad—told my mom last night. Who knows if I'll be sleeping or awake when they come, but here's hoping that tonight is not that night.

I sweep the butterscotch glow of my flashlight back and forth, searching the cattails by the pond in the middle of my backyard where I ate lunch earlier today. *Did I lose the ancient arrowhead here?* It's black. An obsidian arrow.

How am I going to find a black arrow in the dirt?

I squint and keep searching. Honestly, I don't remember ever possessing—much less losing—an ancient relic gifted to me by a prince. I'm not exactly the kind of girl a prince would even notice, unless he was the prince of nerds. But I have been a bit confused lately. It's the new medicine. I think.

Suddenly, death warmed over stinks up the sticky air that clings to my skin.

Cattails rustle, whispering a warning. But I haven't found the lost relic yet. I glance over my left shoulder.

Grody. To. The. Max. It's a gator! Heart pounding, I clutch the handle of my quiver. Only one arrow left. It's not ancient. Not special. Not gifted to me by a prince. But this arrow might save my life.

Beneath the yellow sweep of my flashlight, the

cold-blooded reptilian belly crawler cursed with a mouthful of jagged and foul-smelling chompers charges out of the pond toward me. I would've been safer in Evergreen Cemetery, lost among moss-laden oak trees, headstones, tombs, and dead people.

Storm!

I bolt across the red wooden bridge that splits the four acres behind our stone cottage in half. Fire shoots up the back of my legs and settles into my calf muscles and thighs. Just two more acres to go. *You can do it, Danny!*

I have to.

Zigzagging, I slosh through a low-lying area of our backyard. Cold mud slings around my ankles, attempting to suck me into the quagmire. I keep pushing forward while focusing on my goal—home, a place of safety.

At least for now.

An amber glow flickers behind the windows of our stone cottage. Mom's probably still up reading. I grit my teeth and propel myself through the ankle-deep sludge. *Should I scream for help? Never. Wimps lose their marbles, then whine about it.* The beast slaps its tail as it snakes its way through the mud, letting me know that it's still on my trail.

One more acre to go.

My lungs scream.

I'm tired.

Time for Plan B.

I launch my body upward, reach up and grab an arm of a moss-draped oak, then scamper up the stairs of the treehouse anchored in the one-hundred-year-old giant's crooked branches.

"Th-th-thanks, Grandpa." Grandpa Cavanaugh died a

few years ago, but his legacy—a Swiss Family Robinson fortress—remains. It was a birthday gift to me before he took his last journey to a faraway place. A place where more angels live in the neighborhood than people. In my book, it wouldn't be a bad place to move to. *What do angels look like? I sure could use one about now.*

At the base of the tree, the gator waits for me. Hissing. Snarling. Seemingly shouting that my end lingers closer than I think. But if my end has arrived, then what about Mother and Father?

I need to survive.

For their sakes. Not mine.

I check my pulse. Not dead yet. Mission accomplished.

Acknowledgments

Yeshua, thank you for inspiring this book through my imagination at a time when I needed it most. You've always been faithful to me.

Special thanks to my late father, Chaplain Austin Brown; my mother, Mrs. Jeanette Brown; and my sisters and friends.

To my ancestors, thank you for your bravery.

To my editors, Ann Castro and Emily Dings at AnnCastro Studio, Faralee Pozo at Upwork.com, and Courtney Rae Andersson at Elevation Editorial—thank you all for your eagle-eye talents.

To my readers, thank you for loving this story. These characters exist for you.

Author Biography

J. Nell Brown, the daughter of a chaplain and a teacher, is a Florida native.

Her relationship with Yeshua (the Hebrew name for Jesus) is fused with experiences in life, travel, extensive Bible study, and people's stories—all of which she combines to create characters, plots, and settings for her novels and short stories. An involuntary insomniac, Brown practices medicine and writes in her free time.

She is a self-proclaimed nerd and loves all things scientific. Her love of science is demonstrated by her research at Los Alamos National Laboratory, the site for the development of the atomic bomb. She graduated with honors from the University of Florida (U of F) College of Agriculture and received her medical doctorate from the same.

After completing an anesthesia residency at The University of Chicago Hospitals, she began practicing in Florida.

Her heart overflows with compassion for people who are hurting, particularly children. A portion of the proceeds from this book will go to the A21 Campaign, a rescue charity for human-trafficked children, and Eastside Baptist School in Gainesville, Florida, a school of love, values, and solid educational curriculum for children whose parents would not otherwise be able to afford an alternative school education.

Her first nonfiction book, *Shhh, My Father Is Speaking, and I Am Listening*, is about her prayer journey. The Bible is her favorite literary masterpiece. You may follow J. Nell Brown on her author website: JNellBrown.com.

www.ingramcontent.com/pod-product-compliance
Lightning Source LLC
Chambersburg PA
CBHW030403200726
48286CB00015B/2784